The
Winter
Witch

by Clay
Bonnyman
Evans

illustrated by
Robert
Bender

Holiday House / New York

Text copyright © 2005 by Clay Bonnyman Evans
Illustrations copyright © 2005 by Robert Bender
All Rights Reserved
Printed in the United States of America
www.holidayhouse.com
First Edition
1 3 5 7 9 10 8 6 4 2
Library of Congress Cataloging-in-Publication Data
Evans, Clay Bonnyman.
The winter witch / by Clay Bonnyman Evans ;
illustrated by Robert Bender.—1st ed.
p. cm.
Summary: Now that his parents are divorced,
Stephen is not looking forward to Christmas in a new home
with his new Jewish stepmother; but an old neighbor
gives him perspective on the common meaning
of several winter festivals.
ISBN 0-8234-1615-1 (hardcover)
[1. Winter festivals—Fiction. 2. Christmas—Fiction.
3. Stepfamilies—Fiction.]
I. Bender, Robert, ill. II. Title.
PZ7.E8739Wi 2005
[E]—dc22
2004054191
ISBN-13: 978-0-8234-1615-8
ISBN-10: 0-8234-1615-1

This book is for Jody,
my source of light in every season,
and in memory of Hobo, forever friend,
who was always by my side,
come rain, snow, or dark of night. I miss you.

Thanks to my former editor and publisher Colleen Conant
for inspiring me to write this story. Thanks also to Pam Penfold:
a witch she isn't, but her house and pond in Fourmile Canyon—
and the wonderful denizens who live nearby—
gave me the setting for this story.
C. B. E.

For Sophie, our little light that glows bright
. . . and special thanks to Ellen and Hugh
R. B.

"Dewey, no!" Stephen hissed. His dog had cornered Polly, his stepmother's cat, again. But it was too late.

"Stephen, put Dewey outside."

"But, Dad, it's Christmas!"

"Until he learns to behave himself, he'll have to stay outside. Polly was here first, remember."

This was the worst Christmas ever. Stephen still wasn't used to his new house in the mountains, where he and his sister, Sarah, had moved in November, after his dad had married Deborah. And Dewey kept getting into trouble with Polly.

Stephen pulled Dewey toward the front door and looked across the room, where his twelve-year-old sister was on the couch, giggling with their new stepbrother, Ari. Stephen frowned at the golden, branched menorah over the fireplace, near the Christmas tree.

"I'm going outside," Stephen called.

"Don't go far," his father said.

"And beware of the witch!" Ari said. Sarah laughed.

Stephen set out across the deep, fresh snow with Dewey beside him. The moon and a million stars shone down.

Stephen wasn't scared. Ari was just teasing about the woman who lived in the house by the pond. Stephen knew there weren't real witches. At least he was pretty sure.

"Right?" he asked Dewey, who only barked and spun circles in the snow, tail wagging.

Following the creek, they came to a steep bank. Dewey bounded ahead, but as Stephen climbed up behind, he slipped and tumbled down. He came up spluttering, wearing a beard of snow.

"I *hate* Christmas!" he shouted.

"Can it be?" came a reply. "A boy who hates Christmas?"

Stephen scrambled to his feet and saw the bent figure of an old woman above him next to Dewey. So there *was* a witch! Would she turn Dewey into a toad? A toad wouldn't be much fun for a pet. Of course, it wouldn't matter . . . if Stephen were a toad too.

"Well?" the old woman said.

"I . . . fell," Stephen said.

"Hmph. I fall too, but I don't let it ruin my day, much less Christmas!" The witch paused. "You're on my land, you know."

"I'm sorry," Stephen mumbled. "We'll go."

"Not so fast!" she snapped. "I'm not through with you."

Stephen began to back away, wide-eyed, but a tree root reached out and tripped him. Or so it seemed. The witch cackled.

"Now then, Dewey, what's this boy's name?" The dog danced around her feet and barked. "Eh? Didn't catch that."

"It's Stephen," the boy answered.

"Stephen. Well. And I," said the witch, "am Mathilda. But you may call me Mattie. Now come along, and do try to keep your face out of the snow this time."

Stephen followed her through trees strung with popcorn and cranberries until they came to a small, frozen pond. A house loomed over it, dark except for a single window that glowed with faint light. Mattie reached for an ax leaning next to a tree.

Stephen squealed.

"Oh, now, don't believe everything people tell you . . . *especially* new brothers!" she said, laughing. "I just need you to chop a hole in the ice. About there, about so big. Go on! When you've finished, we'll go inside and warm up."

Stephen chopped till his heart beat hard, till black water reflected starlight. His nose felt like a frozen raspberry as he followed Mattie to the house.

"What about Dewey?" he asked.

"Bring him in," Mattie said.

"Do you have any . . . cats?" Stephen asked. Witches were supposed to keep black cats, weren't they?

"More than I can count," Mattie said, grinning. "But your pooch won't bother 'em. They'll see to that."

Inside, the house was cozy and warm. Cats *were* everywhere: draped across chairs, curled up on the sofa, stretched out before a glowing log in the fireplace. Dewey sniffed at a cat and got a quick paw to the snout. He backed away with a yelp.

"He'll learn soon enough!" Mattie cackled in the kitchen. Sure enough, Dewey turned three circles and lay down before the fire with a grunt—right next to a cat.

"I don't put up a tree," Mattie said, handing Stephen a steaming cup. "Just popcorn and berries on the trees outside, for the birds and squirrels. I have a man bring me my Yule log."

"It's neat," Stephen said. The cocoa was sweet and hot.

"Now you can't *really* hate Christmas," Mattie said.

"This year I do," Stephen said. He told her about his parents' divorce, his new family, how Deborah had cooked a salmon that day—a *fish*! For Christmas! "With Mom and Dad we used to have the best Christmases, turkey and everything. Now Mom lives in California, where it doesn't even snow. And Deborah and Ari have Hanukkah."

The old woman nodded, then put down her cup. "Come with me," she said. Stephen followed her across the room to the big window. He peered out into the moonlight and gasped. There, by the hole he'd cut in the ice, crouched a sleek mountain lion.

"Isn't she lovely? She comes to drink," Mattie whispered as the lioness glided away into the trees. "Now . . . watch!"

One by one, a fox pranced up to the pond, then two deer stepping daintily, a raccoon waddling, a rabbit hopping, and three black crows fluttering. Each drank, then went on its way.

"It's my little Yule gift to them," Mattie said.

Stephen closed his eyes hard, hoping he'd never forget. This was a Christmas gift that could not be lost, hidden by a teasing stepbrother, or misplaced by a googly eyed older sister.

"You see," Mattie said, "it's a dark, cold time for all God's creatures. And no matter what you call it—Christmas, Hanukkah, Yule, or just plain winter—it's a time to comfort others and shed light on darkness, whether from lights on a tree, menorah candles, or a glowing Yule log. For wild creatures, there's just starlight. But, Stephen, it's all one light."

"And now," she said, "you'd best be off home. They'll think you've been made into a witch's stew!"

Mattie gave Stephen a lantern for a safe journey home. "But I'll want it back. Come back," she said before closing her door, "and bring skates for the pond!"

Stephen hurried toward home. But at the edge of the trees, he stopped and looked back. Mattie's window was now dark, except for dashes of starlight. All one light, he thought.

At home, after stomping the snow off his feet, Stephen told his whole family about the witch and the mountain lion, the Yule log and the starlight, and Dewey and Mattie's cats. As if to prove it all true, Dewey approached Polly, wagging his tail. Cat eyed dog for a suspicious moment, then she wound herself around his legs. Everyone laughed.

Before going to bed, Stephen stood by the stairs and called, "Merry Christmas, everyone . . . *and* Happy Hanukkah!"

And lying beneath his warm covers, he silently wished Mattie a Happy Yule. Then, with both Dewey and Polly curled at his feet, Stephen fell asleep, and dreamed of starlight.